Bella Eve
(Believe)

The Bounce-Back Dog
A Puppy's Journey of Resiliency
By Kasey Crawford Kellem

Halo
Publishing International

ISBN 13: 978-1-61244-419-2
Library of Congress Control Number:2015951492

Printed in the United States of America

Published by Halo Publishing International
1100 NW Loop 410
Suite 700 - 176
San Antonio, Texas 78213
Toll Free 1-877-705-9647
www.halopublishing.com
www.holapublishing.com
e-mail: contact@halopublishing.com

To Craig,
We love and miss you!

Love,
Bella and Mommy

My name is Bella and I have faced a lot of challenges and losses. I accept and bounce back from all that happens in my life.

I hope I can inspire you to get through your life no matter what obstacles you face.

My three siblings and I were born on
August 21st, 2013 in a poor, dangerous neighborhood.
My first mom and dad did not feed us or
keep us safe, so the police took us away
when we were four weeks old.

We stayed in a rescue center known as the Cleveland Animal Protective League (APL) for six weeks. The friendly caregivers named me Stuffing, and my other siblings were named Turkey, Cranberry, and Sweet Potato. The caregivers fed, walked and kept us safe, but I needed and wanted to be adopted by a nice family and live in a warm, loving home.

6

In the late fall, when I was ten weeks old,
I was adopted by a kind, caring family who
lived in a safe neighborhood. It was difficult
to leave my brothers and sisters, but I knew
I was going to be in good care.

The family named me Bella Eve which sounds like Believe—their motto and way of life. They always believed life would get better. I started to believe they were right!

I was a birthday gift to my daddy who had cancer. He spent a lot of time at home sleeping and sitting in his favorite chair. I kept him company and comforted him with lots of puppy kisses. Feeling loved helps a person heal.

I was so grateful to have a new home with a big back yard to run around, play and even relax. Finding ways to relax during stressful times is important.

10

I even had my own bedroom which was a "dream come true." Having dreams helps you get through difficult situations in life.

Sometimes I liked to play games with my mommy and hide in her car. We laughed a lot which also helped us cope with Daddy's illness.

12

A few people did not like me and judged me because I was a pit bull. Some pit bulls have hurt people so they are scared I will hurt them, too. It makes me sad when they judge me because of my breed.

My mommy worked and was gone during the day, but she walked me daily, fed me and took care of my personal needs. Daddy was too sick to take care of me, but I knew he loved me very much.

14

In the spring, my daddy had to go to a
clinic far away because he was very sick.
I had to stay with my friend for a month.
I was scared and confused, but I believed
everything would be okay and I was right.
They came back and I went home again.

I knew my daddy wasn't well, but my mommy helped me keep busy, have fun and relax.

A few times I made poor choices because
I wanted attention, but I quickly learned
to be good and stay strong because that
is what Daddy and Mommy would want.

Mommy dressed me up to keep Daddy and her amused and entertained. I loved the attention and having my picture taken. Even though my daddy was sick, we still had fun. It is important to laugh during difficult times.

18

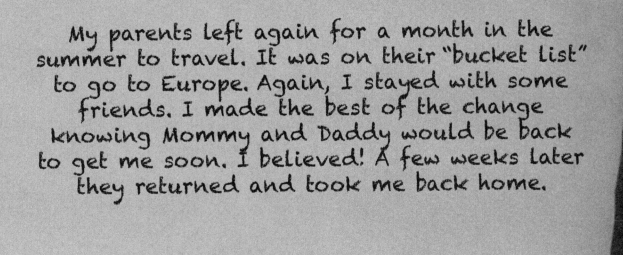

My parents left again for a month in the summer to travel. It was on their "bucket list" to go to Europe. Again, I stayed with some friends. I made the best of the change knowing Mommy and Daddy would be back to get me soon. I believed! A few weeks later they returned and took me back home.

I liked to play with my daddy in the pool.
I believed each day with daddy was a good day!

My daddy had to go to the hospital in the fall. I was scared when the ambulance came to my home and took him away. He spent many months in and out of the hospital and a nursing home. The cancer was breaking his bones and he had a lot of infections.

Mommy taught me tricks. She believed I was smart and I didn't let her down. Even though Daddy didn't feel well, he enjoyed watching me learn. I even started going to school to follow my dream of becoming a therapy dog.

My daddy had to stay in a nursing home for a few months. My mommy stopped working and walked me every day in between visits with my daddy. I took Daddy's place in his bed to keep Mommy comfortable. It made me feel good too. We both missed Daddy.

23

The holidays were difficult. Daddy came home but was very sick, weak and in pain. It made me sad because I couldn't even sit on his lap anymore, but I sat close by to keep him company.

24

That winter, shortly after Christmas and just fourteen months after I was adopted, my daddy died.

I was sad and heartbroken. I cried and reverted to some of my puppy behaviors.

Sometimes I felt like just staying under my bed, but I would remember the good times with my daddy and come back out to play.

Thankfully, I was resilient and bounced back.

Even though my daddy died, he was not in pain anymore and that made me feel better.

I believe I will get through each day,
even the days when I feel a little sad.

I have my daddy's t-shirt blanket to comfort me and help me relax.

I love my mommy and she loves me and that keeps me strong.

I have fun and laugh which keeps
my mind in a good place.

33

I am still following my dream to be a therapy dog so I can help people get through their tough times, too!

I hope my story inspires you to get through any challenges or obstacles you face. Any time you are having a bad day, remember me, Bella Eve, The Bounce-Back Dog. If I can overcome adversity, so can you!

A Special Thanks to the following organizations:

The Cleveland Animal Protective League,
Cleveland, Ohio
-Thank you for rescuing and caring for me.

Elite K911 Dog Training and Behavior,
North Ridgeville, Ohio
-Thank you for your patience and for
teaching me some basic doggy skills.

Marie-Josee Gatian, The Dog Class LLC.
Rocky River, Ohio
-Thank you for teaching me the skills to help
others in need of my therapy services.

Dr. Brian Forsgren, Gateway Animal Clinic,
Cleveland, Ohio
-Thank you for taking good care of
my health and well-being.

CPSIA information can be obtained at www.ICGtesting.com
Printed in the USA
BVOW07*0306271015

422880BV00003BB/5/P